CRANKEE DOODLE

by Tom Angleberger ✳ Pictures by Cece Bell

Houghton Mifflin Harcourt • Boston   New York

For information about permission to reproduce selections from this book, write to trade.permissions@hmhco.com
or to Permissions, Houghton Mifflin Harcourt Publishing Company, 3 Park Avenue, 19th Floor, New York,
New York 10016.

hmhco.com

The text in this book was hand-lettered by Cece Bell.
The illustrations were done in gouache.

The Library of Congress has cataloged the hardcover edition as follows:
Angleberger, Tom.
Crankee Doodle / by Tom Angleberger ; illustrations by Cece Bell.

p. cm.

Summary: A pony tries to convince his cranky owner to take a ride into town.
Includes notes about the song, "Yankee Doodle."

[1. Ponies—Fiction. 2. Mood (Psychology)—Fiction. 3. Humorous stories.]
I. Bell, Cece, ill. II. Title.
PZ7.A585Cr 2013
[E]—dc23
2012001346
ISBN: 978-0-547-81854-2 hardcover
ISBN: 978-1-328-86928-9 paperback

Manufactured in China • SCP 10 9 8 7 6 5 4 3 • 4500743072

For Caryn Wiseman

Town? No way. I hate going to town. There are too many people in town. They all run around in a hurry and ring bells and eat pies, and then they yell at each other to stop running around, ringing bells, and eating pies. There is nothing good to do in town. Why would I want to go to town?

Says you. That's the silliest thing I ever heard. Macaroni isn't fancy. It's macaroni. You know what's fancy? Lasagna. Lasagna is fancy. Lasagna has all those little ripples in it, and then it gets baked with cheese and tomatoes and vegetables. Then you eat it with some garlic bread. Now, that's fancy!

I am not going to call my hat anything! I am not going to stick a feather in it! I don't even like my hat. It's ugly! Instead of buying a feather for it, I'm going to throw it in the trash. Look. Here it goes. Into the trash! It's gone. Goodbye, ugly hat! Have fun at the dump! Now I don't have a hat, so I don't need a feather, so I don't need to go shopping, so I don't need to go to town!

Ye Olde Trash

You could buy a new hat.

Confound it, Pony! Are you trying to drive me crazy? How can I make myself more clear? I do not want to go to town. I do not want a new hat. I do not want macaroni. I do not want a feather. I do not want any other clothing, any other pasta, or any other parts of a bird. I do not want anything that they have in town. Let them keep their town junk in town!

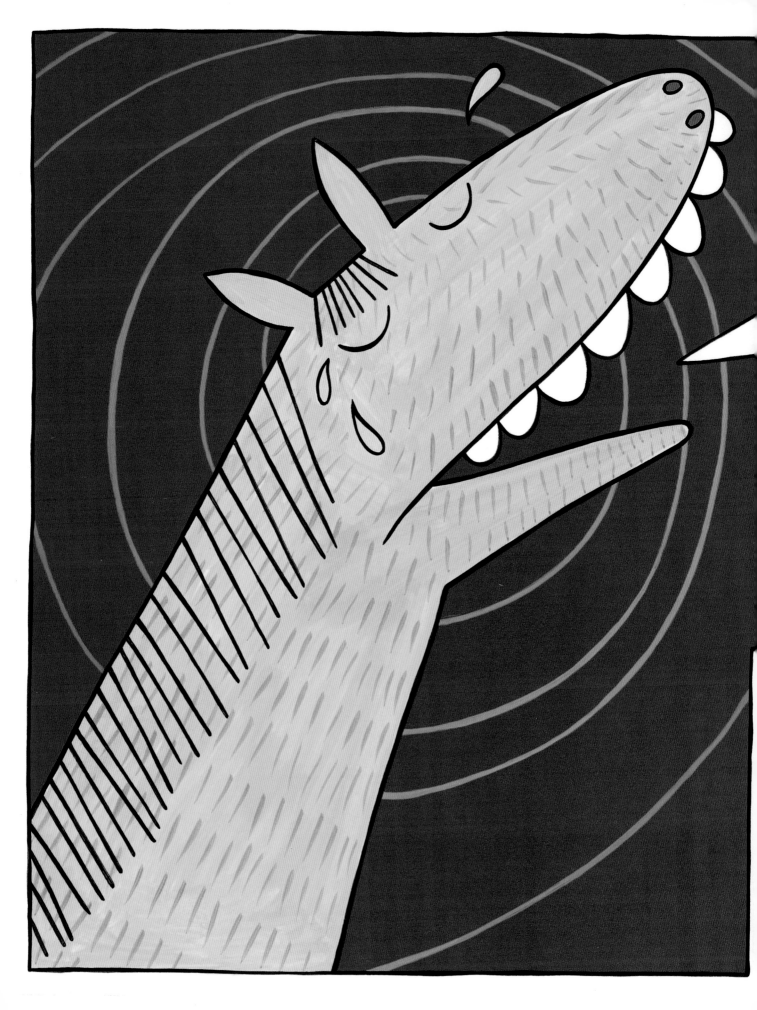

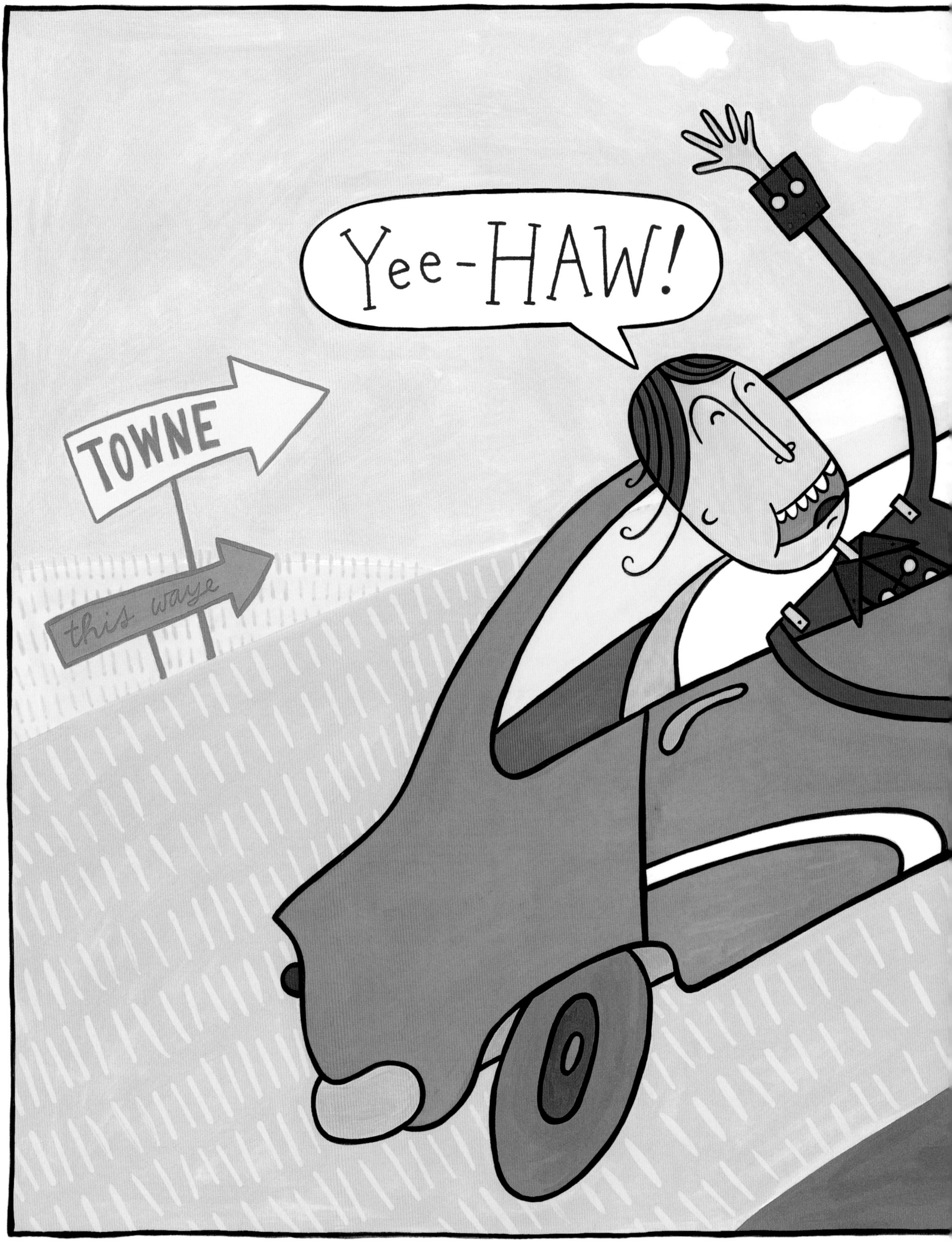
Yee-HAW!
TOWNE
this waye

The End

Oh, my golly, the story behind the real song "Yankee Doodle" is just so fabulously exciting! It all started over 200 years ago—WOW!—before America had won the Revolutionary War and become a free country. It was so long ago that now no one knows who actually wrote the song. It may have been an Englishman who was making fun of the Americans, or it may have been an American colonist with a crazy sense of humor. First they would sing:"Yankee Doodle went to town, a-riding on a pony." (That's me! I'm a pony!) You know, back then they didn't have cars, so the fastest way to get to town was on a horse or pony. (That's me! I'm fast!) Then they would sing:"Stuck a feather in his hat, and called it macaroni." Macaroni really did mean "fancy," but I think the real reason they said it is because it rhymes with "pony." (That's me! I rhyme!) So when you put it all together, it's really fun to sing. In fact, I'll sing it RIGHT NOW! ♫ YANKEE DOODLE WENT TO TOWN, A-RIDING ON A PONY! STUCK A FEATHER IN HIS HAT AND CALLED IT MACARONI! YANKEE DOODLE KEEP IT UP!...